First published in Great Britain in 2003 by Brimax,
an imprint of Octopus Publishing Group Ltd
2-4 Heron Quays, London E14 4JP

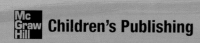 Children's Publishing

This edition published in the United States of America in 2003 by
Gingham Dog Press
an imprint of McGraw-Hill Children's Publishing,
a Division of The McGraw-Hill Companies
8787 Orion Place
Columbus, Ohio 43240-4027

www.MHkids.com

Library of Congress Cataloging-in-Publication Data is on file with the publisher.

Printed in China.

1-57768-442-7

1 2 3 4 5 6 7 8 9 10 BRI 09 08 07 06 05 04 03

The McGraw-Hill Companies

Pirate Jam

by **Jo Brown**

GINGHAM DOG
PRESS

Columbus, Ohio

Once upon a time, in the middle of the deep blue sea, lived a gang of pirates. Well, actually, there were only two pirates, so you couldn't call them a gang at all—maybe just a pair of pirates.

Their names were Fredbeard and Little Jim.
Fredbeard had a red beard, but Little Jim wasn't
little at all. (Well, he was once.) And they had a little sea
dog named Patch.

Fredbeard and Little Jim weren't fierce pirates at all.
They were thrown out of pirate school because they failed
all their exams.

"Arg! You two be useless pirates!" said their teacher.

And it was true. Fredbeard and Little Jim would rather have a cup of tea than a bottle of grog.

Plus, they couldn't buckle swashes.

And they always held treasure maps the wrong way.

Not only that, Fredbeard and Little Jim had no idea how to tie a knot or hoist a sail.

They found shivering timbers a bit of a bore, and they always got seasick.

Instead of making someone walk the plank, they'd rather walk the dog. (This suited Patch just fine.)

After leaving pirate school, Fredbeard and Little Jim sailed around for a while until they spotted the perfect island to make their home.

They built a little house from driftwood and other things they found on the beach. In the yard, they built a shed, where Fredbeard stored anything he thought might be useful. Little Jim kept it tidy.

Once they'd settled in, Fredbeard and Little Jim needed something to do. They wanted to be useful, even if they weren't pirates.

Little Jim tried gardening, but Fredbeard had buried treasure in the vegetable patch, so there wasn't much room for anything else. Then, Patch buried his bones, the tomatoes wouldn't ripen, and the strawberries went all mushy.

Fredbeard tried being a mail carrier, but he got everything muddled up because he held the map the wrong way.

He delivered the wrong letters to the wrong people.

He squashed packages (especially the ones marked "Do Not Squash").

And he delivered birthday cards three days late.

His sword was a problem, too. It accidentally tore open packages. Things always spilled out—like knitting needles, left shoes, and pieces of jigsaw puzzles (usually bits of sky).

Fredbeard collected everything and put it all in the shed.

One night, there was a terrible storm. Fredbeard, Little Jim, and Patch sat warm and dry in their cozy house. They were very glad that they weren't out at sea like their old friends from pirate school.

The next day, lots of boxes washed up on the shore.
Fredbeard and Little Jim went to investigate, but they
found no pirate treasure, no gold coins, no yo ho ho, and
certainly, no bottle of rum. In the boxes, there were bags
of sugar and lots of brightly colored wool.

Fredbeard and Little Jim gathered up the boxes and stored everything in their shed. Fredbeard said it all would be useful some day.

Little Jim wasn't sure he agreed, but he liked to keep the beach neat.

One day Fredbeard and Little Jim had a nice cup of tea and a slice of toast. "It would be grand if we had something to put on this toast," said Little Jim.

Suddenly, Fredbeard had a bright idea.
(He hadn't had an idea before, let alone a
bright one, so he had to lie down for awhile.)

When he got up, Fredbeard picked all the squishy strawberries in the garden. Then he went to the shed and found the shipwrecked sugar. He put it all in a big pan on the stove and boiled it up to make jam.

He poured the jam into jars and drew his picture on the labels.

"Ahar! It be Pirate Jam!" he said.

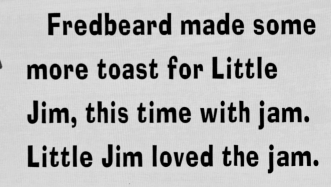

Fredbeard made some more toast for Little Jim, this time with jam. Little Jim loved the jam.

After finishing his toast, Little Jim went to the shed. He wanted to do something useful, too. Just then he spotted the shipwrecked wool and some knitting needles. *Hmm*, he thought, *it's getting a bit chilly these days, maybe I could make us some sweaters.*

He remembered how his granny had taught him to knit years before. He quickly began.

Soon, he had a whole box full of woolly sweaters, socks, and scarves. He showed them to Fredbeard, who had another good idea. (He was getting used to it by now.) "Let's take our jam and sweaters to the market!"

Everyone loved the delicious strawberry jam and the warm, snuggly sweaters. By the end of the day, the pirates sold everything. They took home a big bag of gold! (They decided not to bury it in the garden this time.)

Fredbeard and Little Jim had finally proven they were useful—even if they weren't really pirates.